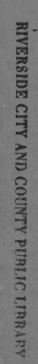

Ruth Martinez

Mrs. McDockerty's Knitting

Illustrated by Catharine O'Neill

Houghton Mifflin Company

Boston   1990

To my parents, Richard and Anna Harston, with love—R.M.

To Gail Kendall—C.O'N.

Library of Congress Cataloging-in-Publication Data

Martinez, Ruth.
    Mrs. McDockerty's knitting / Ruth Martinez; illustrated by
Catharine O'Neill.
        p.   cm.
    Summary: Relates the precarious plight of Mrs. McDockerty who,
with the help of a stool and barrel, climbs higher and higher on a
table to finish her knitting and avoid her fighting animals.
    ISBN 0-395-51591-2
    [1. Knitting—Fiction. 2. Animals—Fiction.] I. O'Neill,
Catharine, ill. II. Title.
PZ7.M36717Mr   1990   89-24496
[E]—dc20   CIP
                            AC

Printed in the United States of America

BP 10 9 8 7 6 5 4 3 2 1

Clickety Clack,
Sweater for Jack
went Mrs. McDockerty's knitting.

Tuggity Roll
Wool in a Bowl
went Mrs. McDockerty's yarn.

Mrs. McDockerty sat on her stool
with knitting in her lap,
yarn in a bowl,
and bowl on the floor.
Clickety Clack.

Cat walked in, *Sweater for Jack*.

She watched yarn
with her head cocked one way,
Tuggity Roll,
and then the other,
Wool in a Bowl.

All at once, Cat pounced on yarn.

"Cat! Yarn! Stop fighting this instant!" shouted Mrs. McDockerty.
She was angry.

Mrs. McDockerty untangled Cat and yarn.

She put her stool on the table, then climbed up.

Clickety Clack
Sweater for Jack
went Mrs. McDockerty's knitting.

Tuggity Roll
Wool in a Bowl
went Mrs. McDockerty's yarn.

Mrs. McDockerty sat on her stool
with knitting in her lap,
yarn in a bowl,
bowl on the table,
and table on the floor.
Clickety Clack.

Dog walked in, *Sweater for Jack.*

He watched knitting
with his head cocked one way,
Tuggity Roll,
and then the other,
Wool in a Bowl.

All at once, Dog leaped at knitting,
and Cat pounced on yarn.

"Dog! Knitting! Cat! Yarn!
Stop fighting this instant!" shouted Mrs. McDockerty.
She was VERY angry.

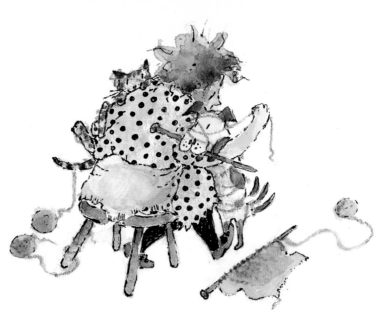

Mrs. McDockerty untangled Dog, knitting, Cat, and yarn.
She put a barrel on the table
and her stool on the barrel,
then climbed up.

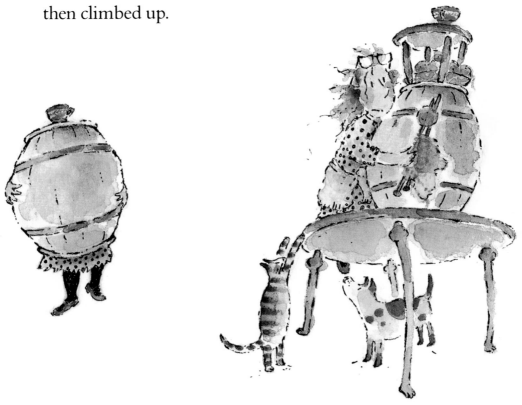

Clickety Clack
Sweater for Jack
went Mrs. McDockerty's knitting.

Tuggity Roll
Wool in a Bowl
went Mrs. McDockerty's yarn.

Mrs. McDockerty sat on her stool
with knitting in her lap,
yarn in a bowl,
bowl on the barrel,
barrel on the table,
and table on the floor.
Clickety Clack.

20

Pig walked in, *Sweater for Jack*.

He watched Mrs. McDockerty
with his head cocked one way,
Tuggity Roll,

and then the other,
Wool in a Bowl.

Mrs. McDockerty stopped knitting
and glared at Pig.

Pig went to sleep.

So did Dog.

So did Cat.

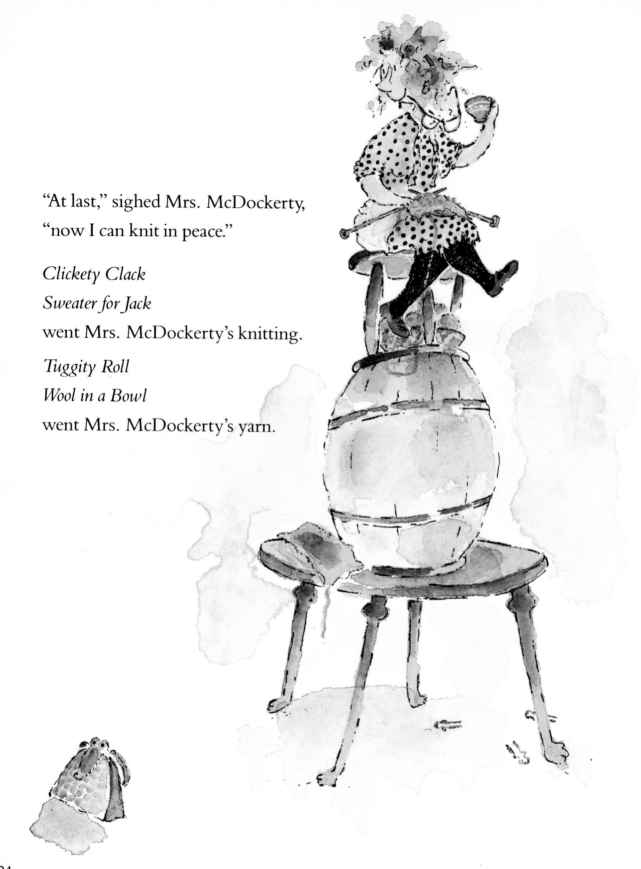

"At last," sighed Mrs. McDockerty,
"now I can knit in peace."

Clickety Clack
Sweater for Jack
went Mrs. McDockerty's knitting.

Tuggity Roll
Wool in a Bowl
went Mrs. McDockerty's yarn.

Pretty soon Jack came home,
but he couldn't get in.
Pig was in the way.
"Move, Pig!" said Jack, giving him a shove.

All at once, Pig ran into the room
and under the table.
Table went into the air,
Dog leaped at knitting,
Cat pounced on yarn,
and down came Mrs. McDockerty.

"Pig! Table! Dog! Knitting! Cat! Yarn!"
shouted Mrs. McDockerty.
"Stop fighting this instant!" She was VERY, VERY angry.
Mrs. McDockerty untangled Pig, table, Dog, knitting, Cat, and yarn.

"Jack," said Mrs. McDockerty, "what am I to do?
First Cat and Yarn; then Dog, Knitting, Cat, and Yarn;
and now Pig, Table, Dog, Knitting, Cat, and Yarn have all been fighting,
and I'm trying to knit your sweater!"

Jack sat down to think. Mrs. McDockerty sat down to think.
They thought and thought.
After a while Jack asked,
"How did Pig, Dog, and Cat get into the house?"
"They walked in, of course," said Mrs. McDockerty.
"Well," said Jack, "maybe, if we ask politely, they'll walk out again."

"Come, Pig.
Come, Dog.
Come, Cat,"
said Jack, politely.
Pig got up.
Dog got up.
Cat got up.
They all followed Jack to the door and walked out.

Jack slammed the door behind them.

Clickety Clack
Sweater for Jack
went Mrs. McDockerty's knitting.

Tuggity Roll
Wool in a Bowl
went Mrs. McDockerty's yarn.

Mrs. McDockerty sat on her stool
with knitting in her lap,
yarn in a bowl,
and bowl on the floor.
Clickety Clack.
"Now why didn't I think of that?" she said.